You can be a
Brownie Girl Scout, too!

If you are 6, 7, or 8 years old, or in the 1st, 2nd, or 3rd grade, just ask your parents to look in your local telephone directory under "Girl Scouts," and call for information. You can also ask your parents to call **Girl Scouts of the U.S.A.** at **1-(212) 852-8000** or write to 420 Fifth Avenue, New York, NY 10018-2702 to find out about becoming a Girl Scout in your area.

For Shirley Lange, my former
Girl Scout leader and lifelong friend
— M. L.

To troop leader Anne Hamby
— L. S. L.

Copyright © 1994 by Girl Scouts of the United States of America. All rights reserved. Published by Grosset & Dunlap, Inc., a member of The Putnam & Grosset Group, New York, in cooperation with Girl Scouts of the United States of America. GROSSET & DUNLAP is a trademark of Grosset & Dunlap, Inc. Published simultaneously in Canada. Printed in the U.S.A.

Library of Congress Cataloging-in-Publication Data

Leonard, Marcia.
    Take a bow, Krissy! / by Marcia Leonard ; illustrated by Laurie Struck Long.
        p.   cm.—(Here come the Brownies ; 7.)
    Summary: Krissy learns many things about self-reliance and helpfulness while trying to earn money to go to the theater with the rest of her Brownie troop.
    [1. Self-reliance—Fiction.   2. Girl Scouts—Fiction.   3. Friendship—Fiction.]
I. Long, Laurie Struck, ill.   II. Title.   III. Series.
PZ7.L549Tah   1994
[Fic]—dc20   94-5230

ISBN 0-448-40837-6 (pbk.)   A B C D E F G H I J

ISBN 0-448-40838-4 (GB)   A B C D E F G H I J

HERE COME THE
BROWNIES
A Brownie Girl Scout Book

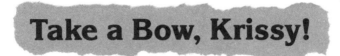

Take a Bow, Krissy!

By Marcia Leonard
Illustrated by Laurie Struck Long

Grosset & Dunlap • New York
In association with GIRL SCOUTS OF THE U.S.A.

1

First Martha Malone walked one dog a day. Then two. Then three. Sometimes she walked them together. Sometimes she walked them one at a time. And by the end of the summer, Martha had earned enough money to buy the beautiful silver bike.

Krissy S. closed her reading book. Martha Malone sure knew how to get what she wanted! Then Krissy looked around the classroom.

Most of the other kids in 2-B were still busy with silent reading. Quietly, she got out a piece of notebook paper and wrote her name.

Kristina Jane Sullivan
Kris Sullivan

Which would be best for an actress? Maybe just "Krissy"! She stared at the letters, trying to picture them all lit up on a big theater sign.

Last year, her Aunt Lynn had taken her to see *The Wizard of Oz* at the Old Mill Theater. This year, 2-B had done it as their class play. And Krissy had been Dorothy!

She closed her eyes and imagined herself on stage. She was wearing ruby slippers. She was skipping down the yellow brick road with the Scarecrow, the Tin Man, and the Lion. They were singing "We're Off to See the Wizard." She was—ouch! Getting poked in the ribs!

Krissy opened her eyes.

It was her best friend, Jo Ann, who sat next to her. "Hey," whispered Jo Ann, "this is silent reading, not silent napping."

"Oops. Sorry!" Krissy gave an enormous fake yawn and closed her eyes again. Her head drooped, then snapped upright. Drooped and snapped upright. She made a snoring noise.

Jo Ann giggled. "What an actress."

"Time's up," Mrs. Fujikawa called from the front of the room. "Read the story again over the weekend, class. We'll talk about it on Monday. See you all then."

The bell rang. Most of the kids hurried outside into the crisp fall air. But Krissy and Jo Ann headed for the lunchroom. So did Amy, Corrie, Krissy A., and several other girls from 2-B. It was time for their weekly Brownie Girl Scout meeting.

Being a Brownie was fun. Krissy liked the girls in her troop. She liked Mrs. Q.—her troop leader, Jean Quinones. Their after-school meeting each Friday was such a great way to start the weekend.

Krissy was especially looking forward to today's meeting. Today they were going to practice for the library Read-a-thon.

The Read-a-thon was held each year in honor of Children's Book Week. Mrs. Q. said it was a way to remind people how important books are to kids. The Read-a-thon would last a whole week. Every day after school, people would come to the library. And kids would take turns reading out loud to them.

Krissy was glad the troop had voted to be in it this year. That meant she would get to read, instead of just listen. It's almost like being in a play, she thought.

After snack, Mrs. Q. raised her right hand for quiet. "The Read-a-thon is two weeks away," she announced. "Today is our practice day. Did all of you bring a favorite story or poem?"

Krissy and the other girls nodded.

"Good," said Mrs. Q. "Now, I know you're all excited—and maybe a little nervous. Just remember to speak slowly, so everyone can understand you. Speak loudly, so they can hear you. And hold your books low, so they can see you!"

Corrie raised her hand. "What if we make a mistake?" she asked.

"Good question," said Mrs. Q. "The answer is—just keep going. The audience will understand."

She smiled at the girls. "I'm sure you'll all do fine. Now what brave soul would like to try reading in front of the whole group?"

Jo Ann nudged Krissy. "You go," she whispered. "You've been practicing all week."

Krissy grinned. In fact, she wanted to be the first to read.

"Yeah, Krissy," said Amy. Then she raised her hand. "Mrs. Q., let Krissy S. do it. She's the actress!"

"Well, Krissy S.," said Mrs. Q., "what do you say?"

"Sure—I'll do it!" Krissy grabbed her book and stood in front of the troop. "This is from *Winnie-the-Pooh*. It's chapter two, 'In Which Pooh Goes Visiting and Gets into a Tight Place.'"

Krissy read just like she'd practiced at home. She used a different voice for each character. Christopher Robin's voice was friendly and cheerful. Pooh's was low and growly. And Rabbit's was brisk, as if he were in a hurry.

When she finished, everybody clapped.
Amy even stuck her fingers in her mouth
and whistled.

Krissy grinned and took a bow.

"Thank you, Krissy. That was just
right," said Mrs. Q. "Now let's split up
into pairs and practice reading to each other."

Quickly, Mrs. Q. divided up the group.

Sarah was Krissy's partner.

"I've already had a turn," said Krissy.
"Why don't you start?"

"Um...okay, I guess," said Sarah. She didn't sound very happy about it. But she opened her book and began to read.

The story was a good one. It was about a zoo gorilla who adopted a kitten. But Sarah read so softly, Krissy could barely hear the words. That was probably because Sarah was so shy.

Krissy touched Sarah's arm. "Try and read louder," she told her.

Sarah tried again. She read a little louder. But this time she hid her face behind her book. Then she made a mistake and lost her place.

"Oh, Krissy," she said miserably, "I can't do this. How can I read to a bunch of people I don't even know?"

"It's really not so hard," said Krissy. "The first thing to do is read the story over and over. A billion times. That way you'll know the words by heart. And you won't have to worry about making mistakes.

"And your story is so great!" Krissy went on. "I love the part where the gorilla tries to play a game with the kitten."

Sarah began to look hopeful. "So what else can I do?" she asked.

"Well, sometimes what I do is pretend my parents are sitting at the back of the audience," Krissy said. "So I have to speak loud enough for them to hear."

"Maybe I should pretend my parents are the *only* ones in the audience," said Sarah. "That way I won't feel so nervous." She took a deep breath. "Okay. I'm ready to try again."

They went through the story two more times.

"That's much better!" said Krissy. And she really meant it.

"Thanks, Krissy," said Sarah. "Maybe I'll live through the Read-a-thon after all."

When everyone was done practicing, the girls formed a Brownie Ring. "I have an announcement," Mrs. Q. told them. "The Broadway cast of *The Secret Garden* is coming to town! The play will be at the Old Mill Theater one month from now."

"*The Secret Garden*!" Krissy couldn't believe it. "My aunt gave me the tape for my birthday! I *love* the music!"

Lots of other girls nodded excitedly.

"Well, if you'd like to go, we can get group seats," Mrs. Q. went on. "Tickets are twenty dollars each. We have enough money in our treasury to cover half. So your families would have to pay for the other half."

"Ten bucks," said Amy. "Time to break open the old piggy bank."

Mrs. Q. held up a hand. "Of course, if the money is a problem, please let me know. We'll find a way for everybody to go."

The girls quickly voted. It was twenty-six "for," zero "against." Everyone wanted to see *The Secret Garden*. Especially Krissy!

2

"Earth to Krissy," said Jo Ann. She cupped her hand like a microphone. "Come in please, Krissy. We have reached your destination."

"Huh?" Krissy looked around. She had been daydreaming again—imagining herself at the opening of *The Secret Garden*, instead of in the backseat of Jo Ann's dad's car.

"Oh, sorry. I didn't realize we were at my house already. Thanks for the ride."

Krissy got out of the car and hurried up the front walk.

"Hi! I'm home," she called as she breezed through the door.

"Hi," her mother called back. "I'm in the twins' room."

Krissy took the steps two at a time. She dropped her backpack by her bed. Then she went into the twins' room.

Her mom was trying to put away laundry. But every time she put something into a drawer, Riley or Taylor took it out again.

Krissy's mom gave her a kiss. "Here's my

advice for the day," she said. "Never try to do laundry with twin two-year-olds around."

"I'll tell them a story," offered Krissy. "Maybe that will distract them."

"Story?" said Riley.

"Kissy tell story?" said Taylor.

They dropped the laundry and turned toward her with big smiles.

"Once upon a time, there were three bears..." Krissy began. And by the time she had finished, the clothes were all put away.

"Thanks, sweetie. For the help *and* for the story," said her mom. "That reminds me. How was Brownies?"

"Great!" said Krissy. She told her mother all about the Read-a-thon practice. Then she showed her the permission slip and flyer for *The Secret Garden* that Mrs. Q. had handed out. And she explained about the tickets.

"So can I go, Mom? *Please?*" Krissy asked hopefully.

"Oh, Krissy," sighed her mom. She reached for Krissy's hand. "I wish I could say yes. I know how much this means to you. But with construction off and Daddy not working so much...well, we have to watch every penny. An extra ten dollars just isn't in the budget."

Krissy's shoulders slumped. She blinked to keep back the tears.

"I'm sorry, sweetie." Her mother leaned over and hugged her. "Listen, I'll talk it over with Daddy tonight. Maybe we can figure something out together. Okay?"

"Okay, Mom," Krissy said in a choked voice. Then she hurried to the room she shared with her younger sister.

Luckily, Maggie was at a friend's house.

Krissy didn't want her sister to see her. She lay down on her bed. A tear slipped down her cheek. But she brushed it away. She didn't want to cry. She wanted to think.

Krissy knew that her family didn't have any extra money. They didn't go out for pizza every Friday night anymore. They didn't even go to the movies. And they hadn't gone on a vacation all year.

Still, there had to be some way she could pay for her ticket.

Krissy sat up. She swung her legs over the side of the bed. SMACK! She kicked over her backpack. Books, papers, and pencils spilled onto the floor.

"Oh, great," said Krissy. She scooped up the papers and reached for her book. Then it hit her. Martha Malone! In the story,

Martha had found a way to *earn* what she wanted. Maybe Krissy could...

At that moment, the phone rang. "Krissy, it's for you," her mother called.

"Krissy! I just had to call!" Jo Ann's voice bubbled with excitement. "Did you ask your mom about *The Secret Garden?* Can you go? Maybe you can sleep over at my house afterward."

"Yes, I talked to my mom," Krissy began slowly. "And yes, I'm going. But there's a problem. Mom says the ten dollars isn't in the budget right now."

"Well, talk to Mrs. Q.," said Jo Ann. "You heard what she said. If money was a problem, we should let her know."

"I know. But I think I have a better idea. I'm going to earn the money myself," Krissy said. "Remember that story we had for silent reading today?"

"You mean *Martha Malone and the Beautiful Silver Bike?*"

"Uh-huh. Martha earned a fortune by walking dogs. All I need is ten dollars!"

"That's a great idea!" said Jo Ann. "Hey! I even know someone who might hire you. You know the Brunos?"

"Sure," said Krissy. They lived nearby. Just two doors down from Jo Ann.

"Well, they have that basset hound named Basil," Jo Ann went on. "Peter Bruno usually walks him after school. But now he's on the soccer team."

"Who?" asked Krissy. "Basil or Peter?"

Jo Ann laughed. "Peter, silly."

"Just checking."

"Anyway—Mrs. Bruno just broke her leg. So I'll bet they need a dog walker," Jo Ann explained.

"That would be perfect," said Krissy.

"I'll give her a call after dinner."

"Good! The only thing is—what do you know about walking dogs? You just have a cat."

"Yeah, but I've walked my grandma's Scottie a lot. There's nothing to it. You put the dog on a leash. You go for a walk. You come back. No big deal." Krissy thought for a moment. "I wonder how much I should charge."

"How about a dollar a walk?" suggested Jo Ann. "Ten walks and you have your ticket."

"Perfect," said Krissy. "*Secret Garden*, here I come!"

3

Krissy talked her idea over with her parents. Then she called Mrs. Bruno and they agreed on a plan. Krissy would take Basil for a walk after school on Monday. If she liked the job, she would walk him every day that Peter had soccer practice.

"Hooray! I'm in business," Krissy said after she hung up the phone.

She drew herself up tall and shook hands with her father. "Kristina Sullivan, dog walker," she said in a formal voice. "I walk all dogs. Short, tall, skinny, fat—"

"Spotted?" said her dad.

"Striped?" said her mom.

"Plaid?" shouted Maggie.

"All dogs," Krissy said firmly. "Even invisible ones." She put out a hand, as if she were holding a leash. Then she pretended that the invisible dog was pulling her all around the room.

"Invisible dogs are pretty wild," said her dad. "I hope basset hounds are better behaved."

"Don't worry," said Krissy. "This is going to be easy."

*   *   *

Monday after school, Krissy's mom took her over to the Brunos' house. Mrs. Bruno was waiting for her.

"Hi, Krissy. Come on in." She waved Krissy in with one of her crutches. "Krissy's here," she called. "Come and say hi to her, lovey."

It took a moment for Krissy to realize that Mrs. Bruno was talking to her dog. Not to her husband. Then Basil waddled into view.

The minute she saw him, Krissy thought of a song from Brownie Girl Scouts: "Do your ears hang low? Do they wobble to and fro?"

Basil's ears certainly did hang low. The rest of him was low to the ground, too.

"This is Krissy," Mrs. Bruno said to Basil. "Shake hands with her, precious."

Basil sat and offered Krissy a large paw.

Krissy almost laughed. Basil looked so funny with his long, heavy body and his short, little legs. I'll have to walk slowly, so he can keep up, she thought.

Mrs. Bruno clipped a sturdy leash onto

Basil's collar. "Time for your walk," she told him. "Be a good baby boy and mind Krissy. I'll see you in half an hour."

Krissy felt very proud and grown-up. She took the leash. Then she and Basil set off.

At first, Basil walked along nicely. But after one block, he picked up speed. It was amazing, thought Krissy, how fast those short legs could go! Krissy had to jog just to keep up.

"Whoa, Basil. Slow down!" she said.

But Basil paid no attention. His nose was to the ground. He had smelled something interesting. Now he was following the scent.

Krissy was getting worried. Walking Basil was nothing like walking her grandma's dog.

"Stop! I mean it!" she yelled. She tugged on the leash. But Basil just dug in his paws and kept going.

Then suddenly, Krissy saw what he was tracking. A big orange cat!

Like a rocket, Basil took off after it—right across someone's newly seeded, very muddy lawn! And he towed Krissy behind him.

"Oh, no!" she cried. She glanced over her shoulder to see the damage. The next moment, she was stuck in a prickly hedge.

Of course, *Basil* wasn't stuck. He was so short he had gone right under the hedge. Now he was on the other side.

"Ouch!" Krissy yelped, trying to escape the prickles and hold on to Basil at the same time. She pulled on her end of the leash. But there was no way she was going to win a tug-of-war with Basil.

She thought about dropping the leash. Then she could go around the hedge. But Basil would never wait for her. He'd run off and disappear forever. She was sure of that.

There was only one thing to do. Somehow Krissy would have to go through the hedge.

Krissy took a deep breath. She put her free arm over her face. And she pushed.

Slowly the branches gave way. The prickles scratched her hands. And her jacket pocket caught and ripped. But Krissy didn't stop. One last push—and she was on the other side.

Krissy barely had a second to breathe before Basil was off after the cat again. He dragged Krissy to a slender maple tree behind the Shady Acres condo development. Her foot caught on a tree root. Ooof! Krissy landed on the ground—and stayed there. She was too tired and miserable to move.

Basil ran around and around the tree. But all he did was get tangled up in his leash. He lifted his head and howled.

"Ha! This time *you're* stuck," said Krissy. She peered up into the tree. There was the cat—cool, calm, and collected—sitting on a branch. It yawned in Basil's face.

That was too much for Basil. He barked like crazy and tried to climb the tree.

Suddenly, Krissy heard a firm voice behind her. "Basil, sit!" the voice commanded.

Basil sat. He even stopped barking.

Krissy had never been so grateful for quiet. She turned to see who had spoken.

It was Sarah.

"Hi, Krissy," she said in her usual soft voice.

"Sarah! Am I glad to see you!" said Krissy. Then she frowned. "How did you do that?...How do you know Basil?...And how did you know I needed help?"

"I saw you from my window. That's my house over there." Sarah pointed to one of the condos. "I know Basil because my dad's a vet. He lets me help out on Saturdays."

"Oh, right," said Krissy. "Well, you sure do have a way with dogs!"

Sarah blushed. "Thanks. I've learned a lot from the dog obedience classes Dad teaches."

"Maybe I should sign up," said Krissy. "I was supposed to take Basil for a walk. Only he took me instead!" She sighed. "Look, will you do me a favor, Sarah? Will you help me walk him back to the Brunos'?"

"Sure," said Sarah. "I'd be glad to.

Especially after the way you helped me with my Read-a-thon story."

Sarah untangled Basil's leash. Then she made a quick gesture with her hand.

"Heel!" she said firmly.

Basil obeyed. He walked close by Sarah's right leg as if he'd never dream of running away.

Krissy couldn't believe it. Her arms ached. Her hands were scratched. Her pocket was torn. And her jeans and sneakers were covered with mud.

There was a lot more to walking dogs than she had thought. And one thing was for sure. Martha Malone had never walked a basset like Basil!

4

Mrs. Bruno gave Krissy an extra dollar. "That's for all the trouble my baby boy gave you," she said. "I'm sorry he was naughty!"

Krissy was just glad it was over—for now.

Then that evening, Mrs. Bruno called. Peter's soccer practice, it turned out, had been moved up an hour. "That means Peter can walk Basil after school. So I won't need you to do it after all," Mrs. Bruno explained.

Krissy didn't know whether to be happy or sad to lose her job. When she thought about it later, her adventure was funny. And when she acted it out for her friends at school, they all laughed. But she still had to earn eight more dollars for her ticket. And soon!

For the rest of the week, Krissy tried to think of other ways to earn money. It was too cold out for a lemonade stand, like the one Lauren and Marsha ran in the summer. And she didn't have enough stuff to hold a sidewalk sale.

By the Friday Brownie Girl Scout meeting, Krissy still hadn't come up with anything. She knew Mrs. Q. would be asking who was going to the play. What should she say?

After the meeting started and everyone had had a snack, the troop went across the street to McCormack Park. They were going

on a leaf hunt as part of a Brownie Plants
Try-It badge they were working on.

"We sure are lucky. What a beautiful
day," Mrs. Q. said as they entered the park.

She gave each girl a sheet of paper. On it
were the outlines of four different leaves.
They were labeled "maple," "oak,"
"beech," and "sycamore."

"One way to identify a tree is by the
shape of its leaves," said Mrs. Q. "See if
you can find a leaf to match each outline.
Then look for leaves of other shapes and
sizes, too. We'll use the field guide to
identify them."

The girls started poking through the red
and gold leaves. Soon they each had a handful.

"I'm going to make a leaf bouquet," said Lauren. "The colors are so pretty. It's too bad they won't last."

Krissy remembered something she and her mom had done last fall. "The leaves will last if you dry them," she said. "You put them between newspapers. Then you stick a big, heavy book on top and wait about a week."

"Can we do that, Mrs. Q.?" asked Corrie. "Then we could make something with the dried leaves. Like a collage, maybe."

Corrie arranged a few leaves. Then she held them up.

"Oh! A butterfly!" Jo Ann called out.

"Can we, Mrs. Q.?" asked the other Brownies.

"Great idea!" said Mrs. Q. "Let's look through our leaves and pick out the best ones for collages."

Marsha held up two big handfuls. "I can't choose. There are so many pretty ones."

"There are so many, period," said Amy, tossing up a bunch of leaves.

"Boy," said Lauren, "can you imagine if you had to rake this place?"

"It would take a billion years," Amy replied.

Raking leaves! That's it! thought Krissy. That would be the perfect way to earn money. Why hadn't she thought of it before?

This plan would work. She was sure of it. So at the end of the meeting, when Mrs. Q. asked how many girls would be going to the play, Krissy raised her hand, too.

"Please bring in the money two weeks from today," said Mrs. Q. Then she reminded them about the Read-a-thon.

"Remember, next Friday we'll meet in the lunchroom. Then we'll walk over to the library together. Wear your Brownie Girl Scout uniform, if you have one. And come ready to read!"

After the friendship squeeze, Jo Ann took Krissy aside. "What's up?" she asked. "You raised your hand when Mrs. Q. asked who was going to the play. Have you earned all the money already?"

"Not yet," said Krissy. "But I'll have it soon. I'm going to rake people's yards!"

"That sounds like fun," said Jo Ann. "Hey—do you want some help? We can work together. And you can put all the money toward your ticket."

"Thanks!" said Krissy. "Two rakes *are* better than one. Let's start tomorrow."

*　　*　　*

The next afternoon, the girls set off. They tried three neighbors without any luck. But the fourth neighbor, Mr. Zubek, hired them.

"I'll give you five dollars," he said. "Just rake the leaves to the curb. The city truck will come by later to pick them up."

Krissy and Jo Ann got right to work. They cleared the front yard quickly. But the back yard seemed to take forever. To help pass the time, Jo Ann started singing a song they knew from Brownie Girl Scouts.

"You gotta sing when the spirit says sing. You gotta sing when the spirit says—"

"Wait," said Krissy. "Try it this way:

"You gotta rake when the spirit says rake. You gotta rake when the spirit says rake. When the spirit says rake, You gotta rake right along. You gotta rake when the spirit says rake."

Jo Ann groaned. "It's more like, 'You gotta *ache* when the spirit says rake.'" She stretched. "I think this yard grew while we weren't looking."

"It sure feels like it," said Krissy. "But we only have a little more to do. Then we can go back to my house for a snack."

"Cinnamon toast?" Jo Ann asked hopefully.

"Uh-huh. Dad baked bread this morning."

"All right!" Jo Ann started singing again.

Finally they finished the lawn and collected the five dollars from Mr. Zubek.

"Okay," said Krissy as they headed back to her house. "Thanks to you, I've got five bucks from raking leaves. Plus the two I got for walking Basil. Seven out of ten dollars. That's not bad."

"Not bad? It's great!" said Jo Ann. "Only three more, and you've got your ticket."

The girls washed up while Krissy's dad cut the bread for their cinnamon toast. They were so tired and hungry, they ate their first pieces in silence. But after a second piece and a glass of milk, they felt much better.

"So what do you think?" Krissy asked as she cleared the table. "Do you have any energy left? Maybe we could rake another yard."

Jo Ann brushed the cinnamon sugar from her hands. "Ouch!" she said. She took a closer look. "Uh-oh. I don't think so. Something tells me we should have worn gloves."

Krissy looked at her own hands. Then she looked at Jo Ann.

"Blisters!" they said together.

5

Blisters were no joke, Krissy found out. They really hurt! For several days it was hard to write. Or play her recorder. And no way could she rake leaves.

At last the blisters disappeared. But then the weather turned cold and rainy. Raking was still out. Where would the last three dollars Krissy needed for her ticket come from?

Of course, Krissy knew she could talk to Mrs. Q. about it. But she had come so far!

Now, more than ever, she wanted to earn the money herself.

Krissy tried not to worry. The weather was bound to change soon. Then she could rake leaves again. In the meantime, she used her free time to practice for the Read-a-thon.

*   *   *

At last it was Friday. The big day!

Krissy filed into the library with the rest of the troop. The children's room was full of people. Still, Krissy quickly spotted her family near the front.

Most of the girls had on uniforms. But Krissy had outgrown hers from last year. And her family couldn't afford a new one. Instead, she wore her favorite outfit, with her Brownie Girl Scout sash and pin—and her great big Brownie smile.

The Brownies took their seats. Krissy found one next to Sarah. A minute later,

Mrs. Q. stepped forward. She announced how glad the troop was to be part of the Read-a-thon.

A lot of the girls looked nervous. They kept clearing their throats. But not Krissy. She couldn't wait for her turn!

Sharnelle was the first reader. She had chosen an African folk tale about Ananse the spider.

After her came Marsha. Marsha wanted to be a ballerina. She read the story of the Nutcracker ballet.

Next Amy and Corrie did a funny poem together. Amy said the words in English. And Corrie said them in Spanish.

Then Jo Ann read a spooky story about Count Dracula.

Krissy gave Jo Ann the thumbs-up sign. "Good job!" she whispered.

She looked at the list Mrs. Q. had

handed out. Lucy was next. Then Sarah. And then it would be her turn.

Sarah was looking pale. "I don't know if I can do this," she whispered to Krissy. "I never thought there would be so many people here!"

Krissy gave Sarah's hand a squeeze. "I have an idea," she said. "Pretend they're all wearing baby pajamas. You know. Little bunny ones—with feet. So *they're* the ones who feel shy! Not you."

Sarah covered her mouth to hide her giggle. Color came back to her cheeks. And when it was her turn, she stood up tall and faced the audience.

At first Sarah's voice was weak. But it got stronger as she went on. Soon she had everyone's attention. The audience laughed at all the funny parts. And when Sarah finished, everybody clapped.

Then Krissy stepped forward. This was it! Her body tingled with excitement. All those people were waiting for her to speak! It made her feel strong and happy.

As she read from *Winnie-the-Pooh*, Krissy kept Mrs. Q.'s advice in mind. She spoke in a loud, clear voice. She held her book low. And she remembered to look up and smile now and then.

The audience really liked the way she did the different voices. The grown-ups grinned. And the kids giggled. Especially when she did Pooh's voice. He sounded gruff and growly, but sweet and cuddly, too.

When Krissy finished, the applause was loud and long. She sat down glowing. She felt tired and full of energy, all at the same time.

The rest of the Read-a-thon went by in a blur. After it was over, Krissy's parents met her with hugs and kisses. And Maggie said loudly, for everyone to hear, "That's my sister!"

As her parents turned to talk to friends, Krissy noticed a dark-haired woman standing nearby. The woman had a new baby in a blue corduroy carrier which she wore against her chest. And she held a little girl by the hand.

The girl looked younger than Maggie— maybe four years old. And she held a long white cane. Krissy knew what that meant. She was blind.

Krissy tried not to stare. She had seen grown-ups who were blind. But never a kid. Then Krissy realized that the woman was coming toward her.

"Excuse me," said the woman. "My name is Ellen MacBeth. This is Kate. And this is David." She patted the baby's back.

"Hi," said Krissy. "Pleased to meet you."

"It's her!" Kate tugged on her mother's hand. "I can tell by her voice."

"Kate enjoyed your reading so much, she wanted to meet you," Mrs. MacBeth explained.

Krissy smiled at Kate. Then she remembered that Kate couldn't see. "Um, thanks," she said. "I'm glad you liked it."

"You were the best reader," said Kate. "The way you did Piglet was so funny!"

"Kate loves listening to stories," said Mrs. MacBeth.

"Uh-huh," said Kate. "I have a whole bunch of story tapes. But real people voices are better. Mommy and Daddy read to me a lot. Only some days they don't have much time."

Suddenly, Krissy had an idea. "Would you like *me* to read to you sometime, Kate?" She looked quickly at Mrs. MacBeth. "I mean, if it's okay with your mom."

"Oh, yes!" said Kate. She squeezed her mother's hand. "Please, Mom. Please!"

"That's a lovely idea," said Mrs. MacBeth. "Let me talk it over with your parents."

Krissy introduced Mrs. MacBeth to her mom and dad. They agreed that Krissy could come over the very next day to read to Kate.

Soon after that, it was time to go home.

"Your mom and I are so proud of you, Krissy," her dad said as they got in the car. "Not just because of your performance. But also because you offered to read to Kate. That was a very nice thing to do."

Krissy smiled and shrugged. Being a Brownie Girl Scout meant doing nice things for people.

"I think reading to Kate will be fun," she said.

6

Krissy felt jittery and shy. She was afraid she wouldn't know what to say. It was kind of like stage fright. The funny thing was, she wasn't even going on stage. She was just on her way to Kate's house.

At the library, Krissy had felt good about offering to read to Kate. But overnight she'd had second thoughts.

"I've never spent time with a blind person before," Krissy said as her mom drove her to the MacBeths' house. "What do I do? What do I say?"

"The same things you say and do when you're with Maggie," said her mom. "Kate can't see. But otherwise, she's just like your sister."

"That's a scary thought," said Krissy.

Her mother smiled. "You know what I mean. She's an ordinary kid. Just treat her that way. She'll let you know if she needs help. Or if there's something she wants you to do."

Krissy thought of her mom's words as she climbed the wooden steps to the MacBeths' house. Then, before she could knock, the door flew open. And there was Kate, all smiles. Mrs. MacBeth followed close behind.

"Krissy?" said Kate. "It's you, isn't it?"

Krissy was shocked. "How did you know?"

"I listened for your footsteps," said Kate.

"Come on in, Krissy," said Mrs. MacBeth. "Let me take your jacket."

"Can I show her my room, Mom?" asked Kate.

"Sure," said Mrs. MacBeth. "Now would be a good time. Then when I bring David up for his nap, Krissy can read to you downstairs. Or out on the deck. It's such a beautiful day."

Kate led the way upstairs to her bedroom. Her hand rested lightly on the banister. But she didn't stop or stumble on the steps.

"Nice room," said Krissy. "You're a lot neater than my sister Maggie!"

"It's easier to find stuff that way," said Kate. She trailed her hand along the edge of a shelf until she touched a covered box.

"Here. This is something I wanted to

show you. My treasure box."

She sat on the floor and opened the lid.

Krissy peeked inside. What she saw didn't look like treasure. Just ordinary stuff.

One by one, Kate took each object out and said what it was. "Marble. Powder puff. Plastic purse. Pine cone...."

"How can you tell what stuff is if you can't see it?" Krissy blurted out. Then she blushed, afraid she'd said the wrong thing.

But Kate didn't seem to mind. "I can't see. But I can feel," she said. "These are my touching treasures. Mom and Dad add new things all the time. And I get to figure out what they are."

She moved the box toward Krissy. "Here. Do you want a turn? Close your eyes. Take something and try to figure out what it is."

Krissy closed her eyes. She picked up a piece of material. "Soft. Kind of velvety. But ribbed. It must be corduroy!"

She picked up something else. "Smooth. Light. Sort of round. But with a hole on one side." She shook her head. "This is tricky. I can't figure out what it is."

"Let me try," said Kate.

Krissy opened her eyes and handed the object to Kate.

Kate's fingers traced it lightly. "This is a new treasure. Is it some kind of shell?"

"Yes! It's a snail shell," said Krissy. "Can I try again? This is fun."

Suddenly Krissy realized that she wasn't nervous anymore. Being with Kate was easy.

The girls played with the treasure box until Mrs. MacBeth brought David up for his nap. Then they gathered up a stack of books and went to sit on the deck.

"What should I read first?" asked Krissy.

"You choose," said Kate. She settled into her chair. She had a big smile on her face.

Krissy chose a Dr. Seuss book first. Then a story about Curious George. She had fun making up different voices for each character. And even more fun seeing what a good time Kate was having.

When Krissy came to a book describing all the changes of the seasons, Kate listened very carefully. Then she turned her face toward the late afternoon sun.

"I like fall," she said. "It smells good."

Krissy sniffed. "You're right," she said, surprised. "I never really noticed before."

"I smell wood smoke. And the flowers in the planter," said Kate. "But mostly I smell leaves. The big ones that fall from the trees by the fence. I forget their name. Sick...sick..."

"Sycamore," said Krissy. "We learned it in Brownies when we went on a leaf hunt."

She picked up two of the big leaves. One for herself and one for Kate. Then she closed her eyes. She wanted to touch and smell the leaf the way Kate would.

Just then, Mrs. MacBeth brought a tray onto the deck.

"Mmmm," said Kate. "I smell hot apple cider."

"There's pumpkin bread, too. Kate helped make it," Mrs. MacBeth told Krissy.

"I did the mixing part," Kate said proudly.

"*And* the tasting part," teased her mom. She handed Krissy a mug. "I thought you might like a break. Kate will listen to stories forever."

"I don't mind," said Krissy. "Reading to Kate is fun for me, too. I'd like to do it again sometime, if that's okay."

"Yes!" shouted Kate.

"Terrific!" said Mrs. MacBeth. "We'd love to have you, anytime you want to come."

"How about this week—after school?" suggested Krissy.

"Really?" asked Kate.

"Sure!"

Then suddenly Krissy remembered something. Her ticket money was due on Friday. And she still had three more dollars to earn.

Krissy's shoulders drooped. "I'm sorry, Kate," she said sadly. "I just realized. I can't come this week."

She explained how she was trying to earn enough to go to *The Secret Garden* with her troop. "If I can just find another yard to rake this week, I think I'll make it."

Kate sighed. She looked very disappointed. But Mrs. MacBeth smiled. "Well, Krissy.

If you need a leaf-raking job, you've come to the right place! I've been meaning to clean up this backyard for weeks."

"The sycamore leaves!" exclaimed Kate.

Krissy looked around. The MacBeths' yard was *full* of leaves. But she had been so interested in "seeing" them the way Kate did, she hadn't even thought about raking them.

"Would five dollars be enough?" asked Mrs. MacBeth.

"That would be great! I'd even do it for three," Krissy told her. "I could start today if you like."

"And I could help," said Kate.

Mrs. MacBeth squeezed her daughter's hand. "Let's get out the rakes!"

7

Krissy clutched her theater program. "I'm so excited, Jo Ann. I can't believe I'm actually going to see *The Secret Garden*."

"I can," said Jo Ann. "You earned it!"

"With a lot of help from you—and the MacBeths." Krissy smiled.

So much had happened since Mrs. Q. had made the announcement about the play! Krissy thought about her adventure with Basil. And the fun she'd had raking leaves with Jo Ann. And she thought about Kate.

She's an ordinary kid. Treat her that way.
That had been her mom's advice. And it
had worked! But her mom had been wrong
about one thing. Kate was not ordinary. She
was special.

For a moment, Krissy closed her eyes to
"see" the way Kate would. She felt the
velvety fabric of her theater seat. She
smelled the flowery scent of someone's
perfume. She heard the orchestra warming
up. And the *tap-tap* of the conductor's baton.

Then she opened her eyes. This was the
moment she'd been waiting for.

I'm going to remember everything, Krissy
promised herself. Not only for me. But for
Kate, too. Then the curtain
opened and the play began.

Girl Scout Ways

Krissy S. discovered a whole new way of looking at things through Kate's "Treasure Box." You and your friends can have fun "seeing" with your other senses, too, by making a Treasure Box of your very own. It's easy!

- Here's what you'll need: one shoe box, scissors, glue, construction paper, glitter, stickers, and stuff for decorating your box, and 10 to 20 small, "touchable" objects (like seashells, barrettes, pine cones, sponges, pieces of cloth, coins, miniature toys, play jewelry, or beads).

- First cut a hole in the lid of the box—just big enough to put your hand through. Then decorate your box any way you like. Try using lots of different textures so your box will have a fancy feel, as well as a pretty look. When you're done, put your "treasures" in the box.

- Now take turns with your friends reaching into the box, picking out an object, and guessing what it is. Make sure you close your eyes or wear a blindfold so that you do not use your sense of sight to help you guess. Which things are the easiest to guess? Which things are the hardest?